WHOOPI GOLDBERG

Sugar Plum Ballerinas

Perfectly Prima

Sugar Plum Ballerinas

Book One Plum Fantastic

Book Two Toeshoe Trouble

Book Three Perfectly Prima

WHOOPI GOLDBERG

Sugar Plum Ballerinas

Perfectly Prima

with Deborah Underwood
Illustrated by Maryn Roos

DISNEY · JUMP AT THE SUN BOOKS
New York

To Mason,
my favorite little man
—Granny

Text copyright © 2010 by Whoopi Goldberg
Illustrations © 2010 by Maryn Roos

First Edition
1 3 5 7 9 10 8 6 4 2
V567-9638-5-09305

Printed in the United States of America

This book is set in 13 pt. Baskerville BT.
Reinforced binding

Library of Congress Cataloging-in-Publication Data on file
ISBN 978-1-4231-2054-4 (hardcover)
ISBN 978-0-7868-5262-8 (paperback)

visit www.jumpatthesun.com
www.hyperionbooksforchildren.com

SUSTAINABLE FORESTRY INITIATIVE
Certified Fiber Sourcing
www.sfiprogram.org

THIS LABEL APPLIES TO TEXT STOCK

Chapter 1

I look at my new set of felt-tipped pens. There are thirty-six, all lined up neatly in the holder on my desk. Well, they're neat now. At first, Forest Green was out of line by a sixteenth of an inch and Magenta's label wasn't facing straight up, but I got them back into place. So now, they're perfect. Satisfied, I settle onto my pink canopy bed and open my book.

Then it starts. Thumping, thumping, and more thumping.

Then humming—the theme song for *Robo-Knights*, a cartoon about robot knights on wheels who don't seem to do anything except crash into each other.

Then thumping and humming together.

"Mason!" I holler.

My door opens, and my seven-year-old brother sticks his head into the room. "What, Jerzey Mae?" he asks. He's wearing his striped brown shirt, which makes his huge brown eyes look even darker. And his eyelashes are so long they look like giraffe eyelashes. It figures—*he* gets the long eyelashes, not me or either of my sisters. He dribbles his basketball as he watches me.

I sit up on my elbow and stare at him. "I'm trying to read. Can't you stop humming and banging that ball around for two seconds?"

He looks at his watch, the big digital one Mom gave him for his last birthday. "Okay." He stops the humming and the dribbling. Exactly two seconds later, he starts again. "You *said* two seconds." He grins.

I jump to my feet and close the door in his face. I hear him laughing, "Hee hee hee!" as he dribbles down the hall. I yank open my dresser drawer and pull out some earplugs—pink, to match my room—and stuff them in my ears.

The door opens. It's Mason again. He's saying something.

I point to my earplugs.

He starts yelling so I can hear.

I sigh and pull out the earplugs. "What?"

"Can I use your new pens?"

"Well . . ." I say. At least it would keep him from thumping for a while.

"Please?" he asks.

"Okay," I finally say.

A big smile spreads across his face. He heads to my desk, where I keep all my art supplies.

"But there are some rules," I say.

He stops dead in his tracks. Then he looks over his shoulder at me. "You mean, like the keep-them-lined-up-in-a-row-in-order-by-color rule?"

"Yes," I reply. "And the put-the-lids-back-on-before-you-put-them-down-even-if-you're-going-to-use-them-again rule. And the put-them-back-in-the-holder-with-all-the-labels-facing-up rule."

He backs away from my desk, looking pained. "Why do you have to have all these rules?" he says. "*No one* has rules for coloring."

I don't even know how to answer that. Everyone *should* have rules for coloring. "Well," I say, "that way the pens stay perfect. They don't get dried out like yours do. Besides, don't you think pens look better all lined up neatly, instead of jumbled every-where?"

"No," he says. "I like jumbled."

"Fine. Then go jumble your basketball, but you're not jumbling my brand-new pens."

He sighs deeply and turns to leave. As he does, he accidentally knocks over my

pencil-holder, where I had all the pencils neatly arranged by height.

"Mason!" I moan, as the pencils roll across the floor.

"I'll help, I'll help," he says. He starts picking up the pencils and putting them back, some pointing down, some pointing up, until I can't stand it.

"Never mind! I'll do it myself," I say.

He races out the door.

After I pick up all the pencils and rearrange them, I close the door and start to read my book again. It's the autobiography of Miss Camilla Freeman, a very famous prima ballerina. My friends and I all met her two weeks ago. Our ballet teacher, Ms. Debbé, had a very special pair of toe shoes autographed by Miss Camilla. My friend Brenda borrowed the shoes, although unfortunately Ms. Debbé did not exactly know that Brenda was borrowing them. And also unfortunately,

Brenda's cousin's dog, Pookiepie, ate the shoes when no one was looking. We all went to see Miss Camilla to ask her for a pair of her toe shoes to replace the ones in Pookiepie's stomach. Amazingly, everything turned out okay. We even got to have tea with Miss Camilla afterward, which was one of the Most Significant Experiences of my life.

Here is a list of some of the things I admire about Miss Camilla Freeman:

1. She was the first black ballerina with the Ballet Company of New York.
2. She was an incredible dancer, even though she is an old lady now.
3. She is extremely well dressed and elegant.
4. She is an only child. This means that she does not have a little brother.

Unfortunately, only list item number three

is true about me. I am very particular (my sister JoAnn would say "fussy") about my clothes, and I try to look nice. For instance, right now, even though I am sitting at home, I am wearing a very cute pink top and some jeans that fit me exactly right. As opposed to JoAnn, who always wears slobby old sweatpants and baseball caps, and Jessica, who wears odd combinations of things. That's because while she is getting dressed, she's usually thinking about some poem she's writing instead of paying attention to what she's doing.

But I will never be list item number one, the first black ballerina with the Ballet Company of New York, because it's too late. And I will also never be list item number four, an only child, since I am a triplet *and* I have a little brother.

I would *like* to be list item number two, an excellent dancer. However, so far I am a dancing disaster.

Jessica is good at ballet. She learns the steps easily. One of her legs is shorter than the other, and she needs to wear a special ballet shoe, but you could never tell by watching her dance. She moves in a dreamy, graceful way, and Ms. Debbé says she is very artistic.

JoAnn is a natural athlete. Even though she's not crazy about dancing, she's really good at it. She powers through all the moves. Ms. Debbé keeps reminding her that ballet is an art, not a pole-vaulting contest.

I hate to admit this, even to myself, but I stink at ballet. I mean, *really* stink. I never move in the right direction. It takes me forever to learn the steps. Then, when I think I've learned them, I still mess them up. Even on the rare—*very* rare—occasions when Ms. Debbé says I've done something well, I know that my foot was turned out a little more than it should have been, or that my fingers weren't extended exactly right. The harder I try, the worse I get. Some kids mess up all the time and don't seem to notice. I know every single time I make a mistake. It's very frustrating.

And the worst thing is, I *love* ballet. I watch ballet DVDs all the time. I would love to be a prima ballerina, like Miss Camilla Freeman. It's not fair that both my sisters are good at dancing when JoAnn doesn't even care and Jessica would just as soon be writing poems or taking care of all her animals.

Tomorrow in ballet class, we're going to find out about the dances for our Thanksgiving recital. If I were a good dancer, I'd be looking forward to this. Instead, I'm dreading it. It's bad enough being a terrible dancer in ballet class twice a week. Being a terrible dancer up onstage in front of everyone is a total nightmare.

I hear thumping on the door.

"Mason, what *is* it?" I yell.

The door opens, but Mason isn't the only one there—Jessica and JoAnn are right behind him. Everyone says we girls all look alike, but if they looked harder, they'd see that we're very different. JoAnn's arms and legs are thin and muscular from all the sports she does. Jessica's body is more rounded, and her eyes are softer.

"We're going down to play basketball," JoAnn says. "Wanna come?"

Our house is almost at the end of our block, and there's a little park with a basketball court right next door. Mason and JoAnn play basketball there a lot, and Jessica goes with them sometimes.

I don't want to get my clothes dirty. Plus, I don't know how to play basketball, and I wouldn't be good at it even if I *did* know. I'll look stupid enough in ballet class tomorrow; why start early?

"No, thanks," I say.

"You should try it just once, Jerzey," Jessica says. "It's fun."

"No, thanks," I repeat. "I need to read this."

After they leave, I put down the book and stare at my pink ceiling. In a few minutes I can hear the others laughing and playing outside in the park. I go to my window and look down at them. Their bodies are as small as tiny dolls in the fading light.

I think about the recital tomorrow. I wish a miracle would happen and make me good at ballet. But I know it won't. Once again, I'll be terrible. Once again, I'll be thinking about all the mistakes I made while everyone else is all excited and happy after the show.

Once again, I will be a very tidy, impeccably costumed ballet loser.

Chapter 2

The next day, Mom walks us to the Nutcracker School of Ballet. JoAnn leads the way on her skateboard, while Jessica tells Mom about a cute thing Herman the iguana did this morning. I don't know how she can use "cute" and "iguana" in the same sentence. Just walking into Jessica's room at night gives me the creeps, with Herman scrabbling around in his tank and Shakespeare the rat looking at me with his beady little rat eyes.

I walk behind everyone else, partly because there's no point in a ballet loser getting to class early, and partly because I'm trying not to step on cracks in the sidewalk. It's kind of hard, because it's the beginning of

October and wet leaves are piled up all over. Their smell fills the air. I breathe deeply as I skip over a crack that almost catches me off guard. It's not a normal one; it's a huge one that snakes across the sidewalk and into the street. Maybe a piano fell from the apartment above or something. I veer away from the building just in case.

"Have a good class, lovely ballerinas," Mom says when we reach the school. She pulls her coat tighter around her. "Dad will pick you up today."

"Why?" JoAnn asks, flipping her skateboard up into the air and catching it neatly. "He never picks us up."

"I need to go in to the office," Mom says.

Mom's a lawyer. She usually works part-time, but lately she's been working more because of some big case. Whenever she talks about a big case, I can't help thinking of a giant-size suitcase, one big enough for a whole family to sit comfortably in, maybe with room for some furniture and a wide-screen TV. I wonder where the TV could get plugged in, then realize Mom's still talking.

"... It's been very busy. Things might have to change a bit."

"What things?" Jessica asks.

A few girls in our class weave between us as they go up the stairs. Mom glances at her watch and says, "Don't worry, honey. It's not a big deal. We'll talk about it tonight." She

kisses each of us on the top of our heads.

Jessica looks at me. I look at Jessica. Something is definitely up.

"Get going! You'll be late." Mom waits for us to start up the stairs, then turns to hail a taxi.

"I wonder what that's about," Jessica says. Her forehead wrinkles in concern.

"Who knows?" JoAnn replies. "She said it was no big deal. Come on." She leaps up the remaining steps three at a time, and we follow.

Epatha, Al, Terrel, and Brenda greet us as we walk into the waiting room. *"Buenos días!"* Epatha says. Her dad is Italian and her mom is from Puerto Rico, so she speaks English, Spanish, and Italian—sometimes all at the same time. "Where have you guys been?" she asks. "You're usually really early."

Epatha is wearing a fluorescent orange

leotard and tights. She looks like one of those glow sticks people carry around on Halloween. How do they even make that color? Maybe it's radioactive. But they wouldn't put radioactive stuff in kids' clothes. Would they?

JoAnn sticks her skateboard under one of the benches. "We had to wait for Jerzey. One of the loops on her shoelaces was bigger than the other one, so she had to fix it. It only took about twenty minutes." She rolls her eyes toward the ceiling, and the other girls laugh.

I feel myself flush. "Very funny," I say. I think again about Miss Camilla's being an only child. I wonder if some family would want to adopt a tidy, well-behaved nine-year-old. It would be a lot neater than adopting some baby that spits up all the time and needs to have its diapers changed.

Jessica changes the subject quickly. "We find out about the Thanksgiving dance today, right?"

"We do? Oh, man. I'm going home," Al says. Al accidentally ended up with the starring role in our last school recital, even though she had really bad stage fright and her turns were terrible. Until Brenda, Terrel, and Epatha taught her how to turn, Al spinning used to look like a tornado wobbling through a town, wreaking a path of destruction wherever it went.

Epatha elbows her. "Aah, come on. You were *una stella brillante*, a shining star."

Brenda, as usual, has her nose stuck in a very thick science book. I make a point of not looking at it. Her books are always full of pictures of human intestines and other slimy organs, because she wants to go to medical school. She looks up. "Anyway, dance Thanksgiving a for do you do what?"

Brenda talks backward. She thinks talking

that way will rewire her brain to make her smarter. She is very smart, so it must be working. We can all understand her, but grown-ups can't, which can be useful at times.

"I dunno," Terrel says, adjusting her left ballet slipper. "Dress up like turkeys?"

Ms. Debbé appears in the doorway. She is extremely elegant, just like Miss Camilla. Today Ms. Debbé is wearing a peacock blue turban and a black blouse and pants. A shimmering blue-and-green shawl envelops her. She looks as if she belongs on a barge floating down the Nile like Cleopatra, instead of in a ballet studio.

She thumps her walking stick on the ground. "The class, it begins," she says. She turns and drifts up the staircase. We all follow. I watch Ms. Debbé closely and try to drift up the stairs the way she does. I concentrate so hard on drifting that I stumble, and Jessica has to grab my elbow to keep me from falling.

Chapter 3

We enter the studio. The barre runs along the length of the wall, and spots of weak autumn sunlight dapple the floor.

"Sit," Ms. Debbé commands. We all sit on the floor, all of us Sugar Plum Sisters—that's what my friends and I call ourselves—clumped together. Across the room, a girl wearing a glittery tiara stares at us. Epatha quickly sticks out her tongue at her. Tiara Girl sticks her tongue out in response—but not fast enough.

"Ballerinas, they do not stick out tongues," Ms. Debbé says, rapping her stick on the floor sharply and glaring at Tiara Girl. "Ballet is about grace and loveliness. It is not about tongues sticking out like the giraffe grabbing at leaves on a tree."

Epatha snickers, and JoAnn bumps knuckles with her while Ms. Debbé is looking the other way.

Ms. Debbé continues. "Now. The Thanksgiving dance. What is Thanksgiving? What does it mean? Who can tell me?"

Tiara Girl raises her hand. "You eat a lot, and you don't have to go to school."

Ms. Debbé's eyebrow shoots up. "Well, those are some things *about* Thanksgiving."

Other girls offer ideas.

"Turkey?"

"Pilgrims?"

"Native Americans?"

Clearly we're not giving her the answers she wants. Finally, Jessica raises her hand.

"It's about being thankful."

"Exactly!" Ms. Debbé raps her stick so sharply that I'm surprised it doesn't punch through the floor. "It is being thankful! It is gratitude! So this year, those ideas will be our dances. We will all dance our gratitude, our thankfulness, for things we love."

JoAnn looks horrified. She's not the touchy-feely type. She would be much happier dancing the Ice Hockey dance or the Changing the Oil in the Truck dance.

"So," Ms. Debbé continues. "What are you grateful for? Think about things that make you happy, about stories you love, about people in your life."

"My cat," a tiny girl in the front says.

Ms. Debbé says, "Yes. The cats, they are very nice. Good. What else?"

"Ice skates," says Al.

"Bright colors," says Epatha.

"Leonardo da Vinci," says Brenda.

"Bright copper kettles and warm woolen mittens," says Terrel.

We all stare at her. That is the least

Terrel-like thing I've ever heard her say.

"Like in *The Sound of Music*, remember? Where those kids are all talking about their favorite things with the nun lady." Terrel looks pleased with herself.

Ms. Debbé tilts her head. "That is the idea, yes. I take it from your choice that you will dance like a copper kettle for the perform-ance? Or you would rather do the Woolen Mitten dance, perhaps?"

Terrel shakes her head quickly. "Can I have another favorite thing?" When Ms. Debbé nods, Terrel says, "Grocery shopping."

Liking grocery shopping might sound even weirder than liking copper kettles to most people. But I've seen Terrel go shop-ping with her dad and all her older brothers. She organizes everything beforehand—it's more like she's invading a country than getting groceries. She has the list, and she sends all her brothers out on missions to get various things while she and her dad arrange everything neatly in the cart. It's as if she's an orchestra leader conducting a symphony, and I admit that it is very impressive to watch. Partly she likes the satisfaction of getting everything done efficiently and correctly. And partly she just likes bossing her brothers around.

Ms. Debbé adds this to the list without comment, as if grocery shopping were a perfectly normal favorite thing. "How about you, my dear young ladies?" she asks, looking at JoAnn, Jessica, and me.

In the last recital, we all got stuck wearing big fuzzy purple costumes, because we were supposed to be monsters. Al got to be the Sugar Plum Fairy. Even though she didn't want to be the Sugar Plum Fairy, her costume was *so* beautiful. It had sparkles and a big puffy skirt. I still remember standing in front of the mirror with her, her looking like a princess and me looking like an oversize furry grape. I need to say something fast, before JoAnn suggests we do the Dance of the Car Mechanics, or Jessica says we should dress like iguanas.

"Princesses," I say.

"Sisters," Jessica says at the same time.

JoAnn doesn't say anything after all. She must still be horrified at the idea of dancing her feelings in front of a bunch of people. "Oh, man," I hear her say under her breath.

"You are grateful for princesses?" Ms. Debbé looks at me.

"Yes," I say resolutely. I am definitely not going to be a purple fur ball this time. "I am *extremely* grateful for princesses."

Ms. Debbé thinks for a moment, then claps her hands together. "We can put your grateful ideas together—sister princesses. The dance will be 'The Three Princesses.' Lovely." When

she turns away, JoAnn sticks her finger down her throat.

Ms. Debbé continues to ask for ideas from the other girls. Tiara Girl, apparently, is grateful for caviar.

"What the heck is caviar?" Al whispers.

"Fish eggs," Brenda whispers back. "Rich people eat it."

"Fish eggs?" Al looks ill. "If I were rich and had to eat fish eggs, I'd pay someone else to do it for me."

Before long, Ms. Debbé has worked out all the dances. Epatha, Terrel, Al, and Brenda will do the Rainbow dance. In the dance, they will glide around "like you are perhaps sliding on ice skates," Ms. Debbé says, gesturing toward Al. They will also pull lots of colored banners from the sides of the stage. "This, it will be very much like the grocery shopping," Ms. Debbé says to Terrel.

"How?" Terrel asks.

"You will be plucking the banners like you pluck apples and tangerines from a supermarket display," Ms. Debbé explains, as though this should be obvious. "Then you will wave the colored banners around like rainbows. And what did your friend Mr. da Vinci use to paint with? Colors!" she continues, beaming at Brenda.

Only Ms. Debbé could see a connection between banners, grocery shopping, and Leonardo da Vinci.

"Well, at least we don't have to dress up like brussels sprouts," Terrel whispers.

"Now. To the barre for our exercises," Ms. Debbé says.

Just before class ends, Ms. Debbé claps her hands again for attention. "There is one very exciting thing I have not told you yet." She notices that the tiny cat girl is heading for the door. Ms. Debbé clears her throat. "Have I said the class is dismissed? No, I think

I have not. Please sit for one moment."

The cat girl drops to the floor so fast it looks as if she's falling down a manhole.

Ms. Debbé continues. "You all have heard me speak of Miss Camilla Freeman, the very famous dancer."

"Once or twice," Epatha whispers. Terrel snorts. Ms. Debbé starts off each new class term by showing us a very special pair of Miss Camilla Freeman's autographed toe shoes.

Brenda looks slightly sick to her stomach, because of certain recent toe shoe–related incidents. "I hope this doesn't have anything to do with me," she whispers. She's so rattled that she forgets to talk backward.

"Well," Ms. Debbé continues, "some of you"—she looks in our direction—"know that I renewed my acquaintance with Miss Camilla Freeman at her recent book-signing. She and I had a lovely chat. Now that she is back in

New York permanently, she has agreed to come to our Thanksgiving recital."

I feel as if I'm in an airplane and my stomach just jumped out the window and is plummeting to earth. The thought of Miss Camilla seeing me making a fool of myself onstage sends cold, clammy shivers all through my body.

"So we will work extra hard, and practice at home as well. Yes?" Ms. Debbé says.

Given the way she is staring at us, there's no question about how we should answer. We all nod like bobble-head dolls.

"Good." She nods sharply at the cat girl. "*Now* class is dismissed."

"That's cool about Miss Camilla. And those dances sound pretty good," says Epatha as we change back into our sneakers after class.

"As long as I'm not up there on that stupid stage by myself again," Al says, sounding relieved.

"It'll be fun to be princesses," Jessica says to me. "That was a good idea, Jerzey."

I nod, distracted. How can I avoid making a fool of myself in front of Miss Camilla? Maybe I can catch some tropical disease so I won't be able to dance in the show. Maybe I can hypnotize Miss Camilla so she thinks I'm invisible.

Maybe I can actually learn the dance right this time.

Unfortunately, the last possibility seems the least likely.

Chapter 4

"Who wants more mashed potatoes?" Mom asks.

"Me!" says JoAnn.

Mom passes the bowl to her.

"*I would like some, please,*" says Dad.

"You want more, too?" JoAnn asks, grinning. But she knows he's just trying to get her to be more polite. They've had this conversation about, oh, a million times.

"As a matter of fact, I would. *Thank you,*" he says. He stretches out the *thank you.* She passes the bowl to him.

"It's hopeless, Daniel," Mom says. "Maybe we should send her to charm school."

JoAnn stops cold, her fork in the air midway to her mouth.

"To *what*?" she asks.

"It's a place where they teach girls to be little ladies," Mom says. "Your ballet school doesn't seem to be doing the trick."

"Excellent idea," Dad responds. He winks at JoAnn so she knows they're kidding. She slumps back in relief.

We're sitting around the big oval table in the dining room. Dad's at one end, and Mom's at the other. Jessica and JoAnn sit across from Mason and me. During the week, Dad usually wears his tie at dinner. He teaches African Studies at the university, and even though his students wear holey jeans and T-shirts, he always dresses up for class. He says it "elevates the level of discourse." But since this is Saturday, he's wearing jeans, which he never looks quite comfortable in.

Mom, on the other hand, is still dressed for work. Ever since Mason started school, the number of hours she works has been creeping

up, but she's never had to work on weekends before.

"JoAnn, is that your skateboard under the table?" Mom asks.

"Um . . . I don't know," JoAnn says.

"Well, *I* know," Mom says. "Take it up to your room. *Now.* Someone's going to break their neck on that thing."

JoAnn lopes out of the room chomping on a roll, her skateboard under her arm.

"How was ballet?" Dad asks.

Jessica takes another roll from the bread-basket. "Good," she says. "We talked about our Thanksgiving recital."

I look down at my plate. My peas keep rolling into the mashed potatoes. I lay my knife down the middle of my plate to divide it into Pea Land and Potato Land, but some of the peas are already ruined by potato gunk. I've been too busy worrying about Miss Camilla to concentrate on proper pea-and-potato separation. I spent all afternoon trying to come up with a plan to become a great dancer fast, but couldn't think of one single idea. I start to feel sick to my stomach.

"Are you all right, Jerzey Mae?" Mom asks, concern in her voice.

"Yes. I'm fine," I say. I take a bite of potato that hasn't been contaminated with peas, but it tastes like sawdust.

"What's the theme this year?" Mom asks.

"Gratitude," Jessica says, biting into her roll. "We're all going to be princesses."

"Yuck," Mason says. He's been busily building a pea wall using the mashed potatoes as cement. As usual, his basketball is right under the table. He keeps his feet on it like it's a step stool. It's as though he thinks he'll lose his super powers if he's not touching it all the time. "I wish I had a brother."

Dad notices Mason's potato wall. "Mason needs to go to charm school, too," he says.

"Mason, you know you're not supposed to play with your food."

"Why can you play with Legos and not with food?" Mason asks.

Mason is always asking questions that seem easy to answer at first. But then you think about them and realize they're not. Why *aren't* we supposed to play with food? I don't see any reason not to, as long as you keep the peas and potatoes in their proper areas.

"Because we said so," Mom says, a response she falls back on quite frequently.

A skateboardless JoAnn comes back into the room and sits down.

"Now, kids," Mom says, "we need to have a talk."

I'd almost forgotten about those changes she mentioned earlier. Just what I need— something else to worry about. We all stop eating and look at her.

"You know I've been working more these days," she begins.

"Yeah. You haven't played Legos with me at *all* this week," Mason says, staring at her reproachfully.

Mom nods. "I know, honey. But I'm doing work that's important. And you're all going to need to help out."

"We already clean our rooms and stuff," JoAnn says. This is not entirely true. Jessica and I clean our rooms. JoAnn's room looks as though a chain of tropical storms had swept through it.

"Since when have *you* cleaned your room? And that's not what I mean, anyway," Mom replies. "I'm going to be working later on Tuesdays, and I'll also need to go in on Saturdays for the next few months."

"And I have meetings on Saturday mornings," Dad says.

"So Mason will be going to ballet class with

you for a while," Mom says. "I've already talked with Ms. Debbé, and she says it's okay."

I drop my fork, which falls to the plate with a clatter. The last thing I need is Mason running around the ballet studio singing the Robo-Knights song or conking Miss Camilla on the head with his basketball.

I hope Mason will object, but instead he looks like he just got picked to play basketball with the New York Knicks.

"Will Epatha be there?" he says, just as I say, "Does he *have* to?"

"I assume Epatha will be there," Mom says to Mason.

"And yes, he has to," Mom says to me.

"Yes!" Mason says triumphantly. Mason is in love with Epatha. He says he's going to marry her. I think he is mainly in love with her because her family owns an Italian rest-aurant and her mom stuffs him full of spaghetti and linguine every time he walks in the door.

"Why can't he go to Mrs. Whitman's?" I ask. She takes care of us sometimes if Mom and Dad both have to work late.

Mom sighs. "Your father and I are both very busy. It would take twice as long to drop you girls off at class *and* take Mason to Mrs. Whitman's. We're lucky your father and Mr. Lester are friends; otherwise I'm not sure Ms. Debbé would have agreed."

Mr. Lester is Ms. Debbé's son. He teaches at the Nutcracker School, too. He and Dad met when Mr. Lester was researching a ballet based on an African folktale two years ago. That's how we all ended up going to the Nutcracker School.

"But how will we be able to focus in class?" I say. "You want us to get the full benefit of our ballet education, don't you?"

"Getting the full benefit of our education"

is always a good angle to try with our parents. But I can see from the look in Mom's eye that it's not going to work this time.

"Mason can bring his coloring books and his schoolwork," Mom says, plucking a roll from the serving plate.

"And my basketball," he adds.

"And his basketball. He'll just sit quietly while you're taking class, won't you, honey?"

Mason nods, his eyes wide. He looks like a little angel.

I glare at him. He's not fooling me.

"But Mom—"

"Jerzey Mae, that's enough. Your sisters don't have a problem with this. Right?" She looks at them.

JoAnn shrugs. "I don't care."

"It might be kind of fun to have him in class," Jessica says. Jessica is an optimist. (That was one of our advanced reading-vocabulary words last week. It means someone who looks on the bright side of things even when she shouldn't.)

I stab at my potatoes with my fork. "Well, he'd better not distract us or get us in trouble or embarrass us or anything."

Dad starts to clear the table. Mom stands up to help him.

"Of course he won't," Mom says, stacking Jessica's plate on top of her own. "He's just a little boy. What possible harm could he do?"

I don't know. But I'm afraid we're going to find out.

Chapter 5

Al, Brenda, and Terrel are sitting on the bench in the waiting room when Jessica, JoAnn, Mason, and I walk into the Nutcracker School.

"What is *he* doing here?" Terrel asks, staring blankly at Mason.

"Mason's coming to class with us for a while," Jessica says.

Terrel continues to stare. She's younger than the rest of us, so she's actually only a year older than Mason. But she seems like a grown-up already, because she's so good at telling everyone what to do.

"What's he going to do while we're in class?" I ask Jessica quietly. "There's no way

43

he'll just sit there and draw for an hour."

"I don't know," she says. "We may need to take turns playing with him. It won't be so bad, since there are three of us."

As if I can afford to miss a third of every ballet class when I'm terrible already. I wonder what two-thirds of "terrible" would look like. I'm sure it would not be pretty.

Some of the other girls in the class gather around Mason. "You're so cute!" one of them says. He gets a big grin on his face as they coo at him.

"Are you going to be a basketball player when you grow up?" one asks.

"Yup," he says, casually spinning the ball around on his finger, a new trick he just learned.

The girls giggle and clap. Mason's smile gets bigger and bigger.

"I thought he'd hate being around a bunch of girls," JoAnn says to me. "Sheesh."

Epatha arrives, and Mason dashes over to her.

"Hi, Epatha," he says.

"Hey, Mason," she says, pulling off her fuchsia sweater. "What're you doing here?"

"Epatha has a *bo-o-oyfriennnd*," says Tiara Girl, who has been observing the fuss over Mason from the corner of the room.

"You bet I do," Epatha says, patting Mason's hair. "Right, Mason?"

He nods vigorously.

Tiara Girl, disappointed that she's not getting a rise out of Epatha, goes back to applying glitter lip gloss.

Mr. Lester appears in the doorway. He's tall and handsome, almost like a movie star. The only non-movie-star-like thing about him is that his teeth are not quite straight. They are very shiny and white, though, so if they were straight they would be perfect.

"Go on upstairs, girls," he says. "And boy," he adds, grinning at Mason.

Ms. Debbé is waiting in the dance studio. She is wearing a flowing orange and magenta tunic, her hair swathed in a matching turban with glinting sequins.

"Ah. This must be Mason," Ms. Debbé says.

Mason stares at her in awe. "Are you a genie?" he asks.

"Am I . . . pardon me?" Ms. Debbé says.

"Come on, Mason," Jessica says quickly. She takes him over to the corner, pulls a book out of his backpack for him, then slips back into place beside me.

"Sit, please, ladies," commands Ms. Debbé.

A basketball silently rolls into the center of the room. Ms. Debbé's eyebrows rise up to her turban. Mason stares goggle-eyed at the ball, not knowing what to do.

JoAnn quickly grabs the ball and rolls it back to him.

"We will try to keep the ball-rolling to a minimum, yes?" Ms. Debbé says to him.

I don't know if Mason knows what *minimum* means, but she keeps staring at him until he nods.

For the first part of class, we do the normal things. We go to the barre and do our warm-ups: pliés and grand battements.

I stand between Jessica and Al at the barre.

"Other way," Al whispers as I turn in the wrong direction.

"Outside foot, not inside," Jessica says as I try to kick with the foot that's closest to the barre.

"Turn *toward* the door," Terrel barks at me as we move on to our floor work.

Ballet wears me out.

But it's going to get even worse. It's almost time to start learning our dances.

"You all know Mr. Lester," Ms. Debbé says as he enters the room. "He will be working with some of you on your dances for the recital," she says. "Some girls with him and some with me. As we did for the summer show, yes?"

Last summer, Ms. Debbé taught some of the girls their dances and Mr. Lester taught the others. All my friends and I were with Mr. Lester. Between Al's disastrous spins and my disastrous everythings, he had his hands full.

Mr. Lester takes half the class to another studio, while the Rainbow dance girls and we Three Princesses stay behind with Ms. Debbé. I guess Mr. Lester needed a break from us, or at least from me. I don't blame him.

I look over at Mason. He seems to have given up on reading his book and is staring at Ms. Debbé, probably still trying to figure out if she's a genie who might grant him a wish.

"All right. First, our Rainbow dance girls."

Al, Epatha, Terrel, and Brenda gather beside her.

"Now, as you know, you will be making a rainbow, a beautiful rainbow."

Thump.

"Each of you, you will be one of the rainbow colors—"

Thump, thump.

". . . and you will dance around the—"

Thumpthumpthump.

She stops. "Mr. Mason."

Mason looks up.

"You must please stop that bouncing."

Mason stops.

"Perhaps you should watch instead," Ms. Debbé says. "Ballet is good for the basketball players. It makes them graceful. You perhaps will even decide to be a ballet dancer when you grow up."

Mason looks skeptical. But he sits on his basketball, hands propped under his chin, and watches.

Jessica, JoAnn, and I watch too as Ms.

Debbé begins to teach the dance. Terrel picks up the steps fastest. She looks like a little windup doll, doing each step perfectly and neatly. Epatha also does the right steps, too, but they look wilder when she does them. It's as if she were throwing her whole heart into every little move, even though we're just practicing.

Brenda and Al take a little longer to get the steps, but they both dance well. Brenda's always been good. And now that Al's got the turn thing down, she's great. Which means everyone can dance just fine. Everyone but me.

Jessica pokes me. "Look at Mason," she whispers.

Mason is staring at the dancers. To my surprise, he's not fidgeting at all.

"Maybe he likes ballet," Jessica says.

JoAnn snorts. "He's just looking at Epatha."

"All right, ladies," Ms. Debbé says after

they've been working for about fifteen minutes. "Very good. Alexandrea, your turns, they are splendid. I maybe need to put even more turns in this dance."

The other girls come over to the side of the room where we're sitting. Al is glowing.

"That looked great," Jessica says. She stands and brushes off her tights.

"Yeah," says Mason. "Epatha, you were the best." He waits till she sits down, then relocates his basketball, rolling it across the floor so he can sit by her.

"*Gracias*, Mason." Epatha smiles big. "You should take ballet. Then we could dance together."

"Uh . . . maybe." He squirms. "Or you could play basketball," he says, brightening.

She laughs. "*Sí*. That would work, too. But if you really want to marry me, you're gonna have to learn to dance, 'cause I'm definitely dancing at my wedding."

Mason is obviously taken aback by this news.

"Now. Princesses, please," says Ms. Debbé.

JoAnn, Jessica, and I walk to the middle of the room. Question: what could be worse than trying to learn a dance when you don't have any talent? Answer: trying to learn a dance when you don't have any talent *and* your friends are staring at you *and* your little brother is, too.

"Now. First, I will show you the basic

steps," Ms. Debbé says. "Then we will work together on them."

The dance starts with us holding hands and walking in a circle, which even I should be able to manage. But then there are chassés, where you kind of gallop (unless you trip and end up sprawled on the floor, like I do). Then it continues with some pirouettes, where you flick your leg out as you spin around (unless you turn the wrong way and whack Jessica with your leg, like I do). Then there are some grand jetés, where you leap forward (unless your foot slides out from under you as you land and you stagger around trying to keep your balance, like I do). I get more frustrated with every move. And that makes me dance even worse. My scalp starts to tingle the way it always does when I can't do something right.

Ms. Debbé watches as we practice. When she looks at me, she has the same look on her

face that people get when they're listening to someone sing out of tune—they try to be polite and keep smiling, but really, they want to hold their ears and run screaming out of the room.

She taps her stick on the ground. "Miss Jerzey. Do not worry so much about having the steps exactly right," she says. "Watch your sisters. Just try to go in the same direction."

"But I *want* to get the steps exactly right," I say.

She nods. "Yes, yes. But you are worrying

too much about them. Just try to relax. Worry does not help. Dancing, it should be fun. Now. Again, please, from the beginning."

We do the dance from the beginning.

I do not have fun.

I especially do not have fun when, at the end of class, Miss Debbé says, "Work hard, girls. Miss Camilla will be coming by to visit our class next Tuesday."

"What? I thought she was just coming to the recital," Epatha says.

"Also the recital. But she would like to

observe some classes, too," Ms. Debbé replies.

All the girls are excited—except me, of course.

After class, it takes me a long time to get my sneaker-shoelace loops exactly even. Learning the dance by Thanksgiving seemed sort of possible, in the way that people using space pods to fly to the grocery store someday seems sort of possible. But learning the dance by next week?

I must look as miserable as I feel, because Jessica says, "Jerzey, don't worry. JoAnn and I will help you learn the dance."

Okay. I know Jessica is trying to be nice, but this gets my hackles up anyway. (*Gets one's hackles up* was a phrase in my advanced reading-vocabulary class last week. Although I am annoyed, I am pleased to be able to use the phrase perfectly, even if it's only in my head.)

I stuff my ballet slippers into my bag.

"That's okay. I can learn it by myself," I say.

"Ha!" JoAnn says.

Terrel and Epatha exchange a skeptical look. Al stares at the ceiling, as though something very interesting has suddenly appeared up there. Brenda coughs (forward, not backward). Jessica looks at me sympathetically, which might be the worst thing of all.

Epatha says, "Remember the show two years ago? When Jerzey fell off the stage into that old lady's lap?" She turns to me. "I'm sorry, Jerzey, but it was pretty funny."

"We may be headed for a repeat performance," JoAnn says. "Jerzey, try to fall into someone else's lap this time, so the poor old lady doesn't think we're picking on her."

Everyone laughs.

Even Jessica!

That's when I decide that I am not going to ask any of them for help. *No matter what.*

Chapter 6

I'm sitting on the big brown chair in our living room with a notepad. I've been trying to think of an LTDP (Learn the Dance Plan) ever since we got home, but with all of Mason's thumping, I can't think of anything. I'm about ready to retreat to my room when Mom gets home.

"How did everything go today?" she asks. "Did Mason behave during class?"

"No," I say.

"Did so," he says. "I just sat there and I only lost the basketball once."

Mom takes off her coat and hangs it in the hall closet. "I don't think I want to know what that means," she says.

"Mrs. Chang next door babysits her grandkids every day after school," I say. "Maybe you could leave Mason with her."

"I'm *not* a baby," Mason says.

JoAnn, who is sprawled on the couch, puts down her soccer magazine. "Mason was fine," she tells Mom.

"Good. Shoes off," Mom says, noticing JoAnn's sneakers resting on one of the creamy beige sofa cushions.

JoAnn kicks her shoes off and picks up her magazine again.

"JoAnn, have you read the book for your book report yet?" Mom asks.

"Sort of," JoAnn answers. She looks up and sees Mom's stern expression. "Well, not exactly."

Mom just stands there.

"Okay, okay." JoAnn tosses the magazine down and heads up to her room.

"And no audiobook business this time!"

Mom calls after her. Last time JoAnn's teacher made her read a book, JoAnn found an MP3 of someone reading the book out loud so she could listen to it instead of reading the book herself. She probably spent more time finding the MP3 than it would have taken for her just to read the book. Mom says JoAnn is lazy about schoolwork, but in an enterprising way.

As I think about the audiobook, it happens. I finally have a plan.

I jump up and go into Dad's study. "Dad, can I use your recorder thing?"

He looks up from the papers he's grading. "My 'recorder thing'? You mean my digital voice recorder?" Dad is big on using the proper terms for things.

"Yes, the digital voice recorder," I say, enunciating each syllable clearly.

"Yes, you may use my digital voice recorder," he says. He doesn't ask what I want it for. This is one advantage of asking Dad for things. Mom would have asked a million questions.

He pulls a small rectangular device from his top desk drawer. "Do you know how to use it?"

I shake my head.

He shows me how to start and stop recording and gives me the cable that will let me download the sound file to my computer. "Okay?"

I grin. "Thanks, Dad."

I take the recorder to my room and practice recording things and downloading them until I can do it exactly right. Then I tuck the recorder into my dance bag, so it'll be ready for class.

That night I dream of twirling across the stage in my perfect pink princess costume, doing all the steps perfectly. The audience leaps to its feet as I take fifteen perfect bows.

For once, I am looking forward to ballet class.

"Happy today look you," Brenda says to me as we leave the waiting room and head up to the studio.

"Yeah," Terrel says. "What's up?"

"Nothing," I say. But I feel a grin tugging at the corners of my mouth.

As we climb the stairs, Mason hums the Robo-Knights theme song in between basketball bounces.

"Mason, cool it," JoAnn says. "I'm getting really sick of that song."

He stops humming, then starts again, but very softly. JoAnn turns around and gives him a threatening look, and he stops.

"Why are you taking your bag with you?" JoAnn asks.

"I just am," I say.

The real reason is that the digital recorder is in my bag, ready to capture Ms. Debbé's voice calling out all the steps for the dance. I will take the recording home and listen to it over and over and over—as many times as it takes for me to learn everything right. I squeeze the side of my dance bag to make sure the recorder's still there and feel its comforting rectangular shape against my hand.

After our warm-up, Mr. Lester leads the other girls to another studio, while Ms. Debbé stays behind with us. Brenda, Al, Epatha, and Terrel work on the Rainbow dance first. Ms. Debbé has provided them with the big fabric banners to start using in rehearsals. Each of the girls gets a different color: Epatha gets purple; Terrel red; Al yellow; and Brenda green. The banners are on long sticks, and they flutter in the air as the girls dance with them. It looks cool.

"All right, ladies—places!" Ms. Debbé says. She starts the music, and the dance begins.

My sisters and I sit on the floor watching.

Mason is perched on his basketball right beside me, his eyes fixed on Epatha, as usual.

Epatha and Terrel dance to one side of the room, and Al and Brenda to the other. As Ms. Debbé claps to keep count, one at a time they move over to the banners, pick one up, then dance a little solo. After they all have their banners, they start moving together. When they swirl the banners in big arcs over their heads, it really does look kind of like a rainbow.

"Very nice," Ms. Debbé says after they finish. "Good work, girls. More practice, but this is a good start, yes? Now, my little princesses, let us see what you have learned."

I panic. I've been concentrating so hard on the Rainbow dance I almost forgot what I need to do. I fumble around inside the bag.

"Jerzey, we are ready. Please join us," she says.

I switch the recorder on and run to stand with the others.

We gather in the center and join hands. Ms. Debbé counts, "One, two, three, go!" and we start. At first it's okay, because Jessica and JoAnn kind of pull me along, so I do what I'm supposed to do. But as soon as we let go of one another's hands, I'm completely lost. I turn left when they turn right. I jump when they plié. I plié when they jump. I probably look as if I'm auditioning for a job as a clown in the circus, because I do everything wrong. My muscles tense up, and my face flushes. The only thing that keeps me going is the fact that this will be the last, the *very* last class where I'll make a fool of myself.

There's silence when we finish. My friends are looking from me to Ms. Debbé. Ms. Debbé smiles tightly. "Well. It seems we do have some work to do, yes?"

I want to tell Ms. Debbé that she doesn't have to worry, that next class I will be perfect, even if I have to stay up three nights in a row to learn the dance.

"Practice, girls. You must practice very hard," says Ms. Debbé. "Class dismissed." With a sharp nod of her head, she swoops out of the room, her shawl drifting behind her.

Tiara Girl is racing out of the room just as we go in. She crashes right into Epatha.

"Ex*cuse* me," Tiara Girl says, in a tone of voice that says she really doesn't mean it.

Epatha glowers after her. "It's too bad that little rat gets to dance in front of Miss Camilla," she says. "Ay."

The idea of Tiara Girl as a dancing rat is pretty funny, but I'm not in the mood to hang around and talk. "Come on," I say to JoAnn and Jessica. "Dad's waiting."

When we get home, I run up to my bedroom and connect the recorder to my computer. *"Hurry, hurry, hurry,"* I chant as the file downloads. Finally it's ready. I get out a notepad so

I can write down the steps—I need all the help I can get—then click the play button.

At first, there's nothing. Then I hear Ms. Debbé's voice, muffled in the background. I strain to understand what she's saying. When I turn up the volume as loud as I can, I can just make out the words.

And then the Robo-Knights theme song blares out of the computer. *"They are robots, they are knights, getting into lots of fights,"* Mason's voice sings. You can tell he's singing quietly, but then I remember. He was sitting *right* next to me in the back of the studio. And *right* next to my dance bag. And *right* next to the recorder.

I fast-forward and try again. And again.

He must have been singing the entire time we were practicing. The recording is useless. Once again, my little brother has ruined my life.

Chapter 7

Just because one plan doesn't work, it doesn't mean that you give up. Miss Camilla Freeman didn't give up. In her book she talks about all the things she had to overcome in order to be a dancer. Her family was poor. She moved to New York when she was very young, all by herself. She was a black dancer back when some people were so prejudiced she couldn't even get a room in a hotel when the ballet went on tour.

If she overcame all that, surely I can overcome the teensy little problem of being a terrible dancer.

Jessica came into my room yesterday and offered to help me again. But I kept thinking of her laughing about how I fell off the stage. "No, I'll be fine," I told her. She shrugged her shoulders and left. I closed the door behind her, a little hard. It made some of the pictures on my wall jump, and I had to spend the next ten minutes getting them exactly straight again.

I decide that just because I'm not going to ask for help doesn't mean I can't ask for *hints*. I call up Brenda, because she's so smart. "If you needed to learn how to do something, how would you do it?"

There's a silence on the phone as she considers this. "I'd read a book about it," she finally says. "You can learn pretty much anything you need from books."

I thank her and hang up. I wonder if we have any ballet books—and then it hits me. I have the book I need sitting on my bedside table.

I open Miss Camilla's biography to the page where my shiny pink bookmark is. I still have a lot to read, but I flip back to something I remember from a few chapters ago.

There! *I did 500 pliés every day, without fail,* Miss Camilla writes. *They kept my legs strong and limber.*

I take out my notepad and write *500 pliés every day* with my pink pen. Now we're getting somewhere!

I read and read, looking for the secrets to Miss Camilla's success, until I'm done with the book. I learn that Miss Camilla ate four stalks of celery every day. She wore a lucky scarf during all of her ballet classes. She stayed away from furry animals because she thought they brought bad luck. She sang a little song her mother taught her every night before she went to bed.

> *500 pliés*
> *4 stalks of celery*
> *lucky scarf*

no furry animals
bedtime song

I pound down the stairs.

"Do we have any celery?" I ask Mom.

She looks surprised. None of us kids typically come into the kitchen begging for vegetables.

"I think so—let's see."

She finds some in the refrigerator.

"I'll wash some and cut it up for you," she says. "How much do you want?"

"A lot," I say. "Maybe all of it."

She cuts four celery sticks, and I start chomping. "Do you have a scarf?"

Mom puts the knife in the dishwasher. "What's all this about?"

"Nothing," I reply.

She looks at me skeptically. "I have some old scarves in my top dresser drawer. Help yourself," she says.

71

I race up and get a scarf, a pretty one with red flowers on it.

Pliés. I need to do five hundred pliés.

I drag one of the dining room chairs up to my room. I turn it to face away from me and grab the back as if it were a ballet barre. Then I begin doing pliés.

One . . .

Two . . .

By thirty, my legs are starting to hurt.

By fifty, they feel like spaghetti.

I stop pliéing and check the book again. Maybe I read it wrong.

Nope. It says five hundred.

Fine. I am determined. If five hundred pliés is what it takes, that's what I'm going to do.

This isn't really a class, but it occurs to me that maybe I should wear the lucky scarf, just in case.

I tie it around my neck.

Then I plié again. And again. And again.

Before I go to bed, I eat more celery. Then I sing a lullaby Mom used to sing to us.

I sing it twice, just to make sure.

Chapter 8

The next morning, I open my eyes and realize it's here—Miss Camilla Day.

I try to stand up. My legs slide out from under me.

"Ow!" I say.

Jessica comes running. "What is it?"

"I just slipped," I lie.

She helps me up. I can barely stand. I wobble around on unsteady legs that feel as if someone had run them through one of those old-fashioned clothes wringers.

Everything else goes wrong, too.

I go into Mason's room and see that one of his toy soldiers is attached to a soggy, mud-covered piece of red fabric.

"That's my lucky scarf!" I say.

Mason looks up from his book. "It is? I found it in the bathroom. My soldier needed a parachute." He looks nervous, as if he thinks I might explode (which I might).

"How did it get all muddy?" I wail, looking at the crumpled scarf.

"The soldier had to parachute into a mud puddle," Mason says. "It was an important mission. I'm sorry, Jerzey."

I wobble into the kitchen to eat my four celery stalks, but all the celery's gone.

"Mason ate most of it, then said he needed the rest for a science experiment," Dad says. "Something about food coloring and . . ."

I walk away in the middle of his sentence, but Dad probably doesn't even notice.

"Can you hold Shakespeare while I clean his cage?" Jessica asks as I wobble by her room.

I sigh and take the white rat gingerly

into my hands. Then I remember.

"He has fur! He's a furry animal!"

I thrust him back at Jessica. She looks at me like I'm crazy. I run out of the room and wash my hands seven times, hoping I can wash the bad luck off.

Only two hours till class. I sing the lullaby fifty times in a row.

In her book, Miss Camilla talks about how important it is to have a tidy appearance during dance class. *It is a sign of respect for the ballet, and for your fellow dancers,* she writes.

So I make sure that my ballet outfit is 100 percent perfect. Before bed last night, I washed out my favorite white tights by hand in the bathroom sink. Last time I put tights in the laundry, they came out streaked with orange and purple. Mason had left two crayons in the pocket of one of his shirts, and they melted all over everything in the dryer. This time, I didn't take any chances.

I put on the tights and my pink leotard, making sure that the sleeves are exactly even. I notice a tiny thread hanging from one seam and snip it off. I arrange my hair in two poufs on the top of my head and spend twenty minutes tying pink ribbons—ribbons that match the leotard *perfectly*—into perfect bows around the poufs.

I stand back and look in the mirror. Everything is exactly right. Miss Camilla will *have* to notice how perfectly I'm dressed. She will know how much I respect the ballet— just like she does. I hum the lullaby again as insurance just as Jessica calls upstairs to say it's time to go.

Dad walks us all to class—JoAnn, Jessica, Mason, and me. JoAnn leads the way with Mason, who is bouncing his basketball. Jessica and I follow them, and Dad strolls behind us, his hands in his pockets. When I glance back, I see the Thinking Look on his face. He's staring off into the distance, looking slightly puzzled, as though he were trying to remember the name of someone he met a long time ago. This means he's planning stuff for his classes. It also means that if we want his attention, we'll have to holler at him a few times to bring him back to reality. We could probably all be abducted by aliens without his noticing, unless the aliens had a particularly interesting African mask with them.

"Cut it out, JoAnn!" Mason says. JoAnn is trying to get the ball away from him so she can dribble, too. He pulls away from her and dribbles the ball over to Jessica and me.

Mason reaches over to me, and I take his right hand. It feels warm and small inside mine. He dribbles with his left hand as we walk. For a minute I think it's actually not so bad having a little brother.

But only for a minute. Because right then, Mason's ball bounces on an uneven part of the sidewalk and gets away from him. He lunges after it, dragging me along, and before I know it I'm flat on my face on the sidewalk.

Chapter 9

Everyone stops. Jessica helps me up. JoAnn picks up my dance bag, which I've dropped, and Dad races over.

"Are you okay, sweetheart?" he asks, looking me over.

My heart is pounding. I look down at my limbs and move them experimentally. There's a big hole in the right knee of my tights— my once-perfect, once-clean, favorite tights. My knee looks as if it had been shredded by a cheese grater. It stings like crazy. I blink back tears as blood seeps out onto the fabric.

"My tights are ripped, and they're all bloody," I say.

Dad hugs me. "That doesn't matter, honey.

We'll get you some new ones. As long as you're okay."

But it *does* matter.

We start walking again.

"I'm sorry, Jerzey," Mason says in a small voice. He walks right behind Jessica and me, hugging his basketball contritely (a word that means he does it as if he's sorry—even though I think it's better not to knock your sister over in the first place than to be sorry after you've done it).

"I hope Miss Camilla doesn't notice the hole in my tights," I say to Jessica. I lean over and see the hole getting slightly bigger as I walk.

She examines it. "I don't think she will. You can hardly see it," she says, patting my arm.

When we get to the school, Dad walks us inside, borrows the first-aid kit from the main desk, and cleans up my knee. As the other girls come into the waiting room, they stop to watch. Brenda offers Dad some tips on wound disinfection, which he does not seem to find very helpful. *I* just want to disappear. Instead, I feel like a patient in one of those medical TV shows.

"All right, girls," Dad says when he's finally done. "Epatha's sister will walk you home." He leaves just as Ms. Debbé calls us into class.

"Is Miss Camilla here yet?" Epatha asks, craning her neck as we enter the studio.

"Do you think she'll remember us?" asks Jessica.

"Of course she will," says Epatha.

"I know she'll remember me," says Brenda nervously.

"Mason, you need to be extra good today," Jessica says to him. "There's a very famous ballerina who's coming to our class."

He looks insulted. "I'm always good," he says, fidgeting with his jacket.

Right after class starts, the door opens and Miss Camilla comes in, followed by Mr. Lester. Miss Camilla wears a navy blue dress that is very simple in the way that expensive clothes are. It fits her perfectly. She carries a large purse with an open top and gold rings on the outside. She's pretty old—even older than our parents—but she has perfect posture, and she walks like a queen. Her eyes are kind, but they obviously don't miss a thing. She gracefully bends to set her purse on the floor.

Ms. Debbé claps. "Girls, I have the great honor of introducing to you my old friend and teacher, Miss Camilla Freeman."

Miss Camilla smiles and nods. She notices us and winks at Brenda, who looks relieved that Miss Camilla does not appear to be holding a shoe-grudge.

Before I even realize what's happening, Mason runs up to the front of the room.

"You're Miss Camilla?" he asks.

She nods, looking puzzled.

"I have an important message for you," he says.

"Oh, yes?" she asks. "What is it?"

"Don't look at Jerzey's tights," he says loudly. He turns to me, smiles, and gives me a big thumbs-up.

The room explodes with laughter, especially the section of it where Tiara Girl and her friend are sitting. Miss Camilla's eyes, along with everyone else's, immediately dart to my tights. I wish I could dissolve and drip through the floor and evaporate so I would never have to see anyone again as long as I live. I tuck my right leg behind the left one to try to hide the hole.

"Quiet, girls!" Ms. Debbé says. "Now. Please sit in neat rows on the floor. Today, Miss Camilla will watch as we have a *petite* show for her. We will all do the dances, yes? I have told her we still have much rehearsing to do. But as a professional dancer, she understands well about rehearsals."

Just before we arrange ourselves into rows, I scoot over to Mason. "Why did you say that?" I hiss.

"You said you hoped that that Miss Camilla lady wouldn't notice the hole in your tights. I was trying to help you," he says plaintively.

"Well, don't help me ever again," I say. I hurry back into my row, my legs still throbbing from all those pliés.

"So. First the Rainbow girls, I think," says Ms. Debbé. "Ah—the CDs for the dances. I must have left them in the other studio. Why don't you all take a short break—do some stretches. Five minutes." She swoops out of the room, closing the door behind her.

Mr. Lester and Miss Camilla chat as the other girls in the class, the ones who did not get to have tea with Miss Camilla, stare at her in awe.

I feel Mason tugging on my arm.

"What?" I say, annoyed. Then I see the look on his face. "Are you sick, Mason?"

Jessica turns to find out what's going on.

"He's gone," Mason says, so faintly I can barely hear him.

"Who's gone?" I ask.

"Shakespeare."

At first I wonder why he's talking about a dead writer. Then it hits me.

"You mean Shakespeare, *Jessica's rat*?"

He nods.

Jessica looks at him, horrified. "You brought Shakespeare to class?"

He nods again. He looks like he's about to cry.

"Mason! Why?" Jessica asks him.

"Epatha said there was going to be a dancing rat! I thought Shakespeare would like to see that."

"A dancing . . ." Jessica looks at him, bewildered.

I close my eyes. "Epatha called Tiara Girl a dancing rat last class. Remember?"

Jessica starts breathing so fast I'm afraid she'll hyperventilate. "We have to find him!" she whispers frantically. She loves Shakespeare the way other kids love their dogs or cats. "When did you have him last?"

"In my pocket. Just a minute ago. I unzipped it a little so he could see."

"So he has to be in here somewhere," Jessica says. She leans to the left and to the right, searching the floor with her eyes.

Terrel leans over. "What's going on?"

JoAnn has been listening, and for once she looks worried. "Shakespeare. Somewhere in here."

Terrel exhales heavily and gives Mason a dirty look. "JoAnn, keep an eye on the door. Make sure he doesn't run out when Ms. Debbé comes back in."

JoAnn nods and walks over to the door.

"Brenda and Al, go look in those—"

But before she finishes her sentence, Jessica hisses, "Over there—the curtain just moved."

A heavy red curtain hangs at one end of the room, hiding some electrical control panels. We watch in horror as a small bulge works its way along the floor from one end of the curtain to the other. We see a flash of white disappear into the stereo cabinet just as Ms. Debbé comes back into the room.

"All right," Ms. Debbé says cheerily. "Now, where were we? Ah, yes. The Rainbow girls, please. Everyone else, be seated."

Al, Epatha, Brenda, and Terrel look at each other, not sure what to do. Then Terrel stands up, and the others follow suit. Their eyes are riveted on the stereo cabinet.

Ms. Debbé goes to the cabinet. The stereo system is on a moving cart, which she pulls forward.

A white streak zooms out of the cabinet.

"A rat!" Tiara Girl shrieks.

Within half a second, nearly all the girls in the room are screaming. Shakespeare stops, assesses the situation, and jumps into the nearest hiding place.

Miss Camilla's bag.

Chapter 10

In one of my advanced reading books, something bad happens and the author says, *Chaos ensues*. I didn't know what chaos ensuing looked like till now. Most of the girls continue to jump around, screaming. Ms. Debbé calls, "Girls! Girls!" repeatedly, in an attempt to restore order. Mr. Lester, who must not have seen Shakespeare, looks perplexed. Miss Camilla stands frozen, like a statue.

Jessica races up and thrusts her hand into Miss Camilla's bag. She gently pulls Shakespeare out, examines him to be sure he's okay, then holds him to her chest and rocks him as she blinks back tears.

When everything calms down, Mr. Lester

finds a shoe box for Shakespeare. Jessica explains that Mason brought Shakespeare to class, although she lies when she says she doesn't know *why* he brought him, because Jessica is nice even to Tiara Girl and doesn't want to call her a rat in front of everyone.

I have never been so embarrassed in all my life. Leave it to Mason to make our whole family look stupid in front of Miss Camilla Freeman.

When we finally get around to doing our Princess dance, I do worse than even *I* expected. Miss Camilla Freeman is watching. Mason is sitting in the back, holding a shoe box full of rat. My legs, still wobbly from my five hundred pliés, may collapse at any moment. The bloodstained hole in my tights is expanding with every move I make. I try to turn to hide it and end up crashing into JoAnn like a Robo-Knight. Ms. Debbé looks mortified that one of her students—me—

can't even move in a straight line.

By the time we're done, I am breathing so fast and feel so warm I'm afraid I'm going to pass out—which might be better than staying conscious.

"Well," says Ms. Debbé, her voice strained. "We will work on that some more, won't we, girls? Quite a bit more, I think."

I keep my eyes on the floor. I don't want to see Miss Camilla's reaction to my horrible performance.

Fortunately, class ends right after our dance is over. I pull Mason aside as we walk down the hallway.

"How could you bring that rat to class?" I ask. "That was so stupid!"

"Jerzey! You're not supposed to call me stupid! Mom said."

But I am feeling mean and horrible, and I don't care. Deep down, I know I'm more mad at myself for screwing up the dance than I am mad at him, but I keep yelling anyway.

"You tell everyone about the hole in my tights, and you use my celery, and you ruin my lucky scarf, and you embarrass us in front of Miss Camilla!" I cry, my voice getting higher and more trembly.

"*What* lucky scarf?" he asks, but I steamroll over him.

"I wish I didn't have a little brother," I say, stomping down the hallway, but not before seeing how hurt he looks.

I go to the bathroom. I soak some paper towels in cool water and put them on my forehead, because I still feel hot and dizzy. A few tears leak out onto my cheeks. I use a brown paper towel to blot them. The towel feels rough, and as soon as it gets wet it starts to smell horrible.

I hear the bathroom door open behind me. It's Miss Camilla.

My first impulse is to hide in a toilet stall, but it's too late—she's already seen me. She'll probably ask me what I am even doing in a dance class when I am clearly so terrible.

But instead, she smiles. "Hello, Jerzey Mae," she says.

A tiny part of me is pleased that she remembers my name, but the rest of me is so miserable that it all gets canceled out.

She walks over to the mirror and adjusts her collar. "It looked like you were having some trouble up there."

I'm surprised. I guess she's a tell-it-like-it-is person, like Epatha. But her eyes are warm.

I nod. "I get all the steps wrong," I blurt out. My eyes prickle. "They're never perfect."

To my surprise, Miss Camilla laughs. "'Perfect' is a pretty difficult goal to achieve," she says. "I danced in thousands of performances. Do you think I ever danced perfectly?" She fishes in her bag and pulls out a lipstick.

Well, she was a famous ballerina, so of course she did. I wait for the answer.

She shakes her head. "I was very good, yes. But never perfect. We're human beings—we're not meant to be perfect."

I think this over. I try to be perfect all the time, so this new idea doesn't fit into my head very well.

"Sometimes I think I should just quit," I tell her in a small voice.

She turns to face me, lipstick in hand. "Do you truly want to dance?"

I nod.

"Then, my dear, you can't quit. You just have to find a way to do what you want. One thing you might start with, though, is getting rid of that 'perfect' idea," she says.

I just stand there, not knowing what else to say but not wanting to leave. "I am very sorry about my brother's rat and the bad luck," I finally say.

She looks puzzled for a moment, then smiles. "You have read my book!"

I nod.

"I have to admit your brother's rat did take me by surprise." She smiles. "But that furry-animal superstition was just silly. I finally got over my fear of them three years ago. Now I have a pet chinchilla named Edward." She turns to the mirror, applies her lipstick, and blots some of it off with a tissue.

I wonder if the other stuff in the book is wrong, too. "I tried doing five hundred pliés, and eating celery, and wearing a scarf, and singing at night," I tell her. "Nothing worked. I'm still bad at ballet."

She looks at me seriously. She acts like she's talking to another grown-up, not just a kid. "Something that works for one person may not work for another. You need to find your own path, my dear."

"But how?" I ask.

"That, I don't know. I *do* know that if you truly want to dance, you'll find a way. Often the answer is right under our noses," she says.

I look under my nose. There's nothing there but the bathroom sink.

Miss Camilla puts her purse strap over her shoulder. "I'll be coming to your recital. And I'll be very disappointed if you're not dancing in it. Good-bye, my dear."

With that, she leaves.

Chapter 11

I sit in my room alone that night, hugging my knees. Jessica's been shut up in her room cuddling Shakespeare and feeding him all his favorite foods since we got back. JoAnn's at basketball practice. The house is unnaturally quiet.

I can't do the dance.

I can't disappoint Miss Camilla.

What am I going to do?

I have no ideas.

I decide I'd better go get the muddy lucky scarf so I can wash it out before Mom sees it. As I cross the hall to Mason's room, I notice that there's no basketball-bouncing sound coming out of his door. *That's* why the house is so quiet.

His door is open just a few inches. I peek inside.

As I watch, he stands on his left leg and executes a perfect pirouette.

I stare.

Then he does a chassé. Which happens to be the next move of our dance.

As I peer through the crack in the door, he does our entire dance. Or at least something closer to our entire dance than I could ever do on my own.

I go back to my room.

I can't believe it. My little brother—my annoying, scarf-stealing, celery-chomping, basketball-bouncing little brother—is a better dancer than I am.

I'm flooded by all sorts of feelings— jealousy, anger, frustration. But there's something else there, too: a tiny sliver of hope.

I think of what Miss Camilla said. If you

want to do something, you do whatever you need to do.

Even if it means asking your little brother for help.

I cross the hall to Mason's room again. Now he's playing with a remote-controlled truck, driving it around an obstacle course he's made from wooden blocks, some books, and his stuffed alligator.

"Hey, Mason," I say.

"What?" He steers the truck neatly around the alligator's tail before smashing it into a pile of blocks, which crash to the ground.

The words stick in my throat, but I finally get them out. "Can you help me learn our dance?"

He looks up at me. The truck lies on its side, its wheels whirring. "You want *me* to help you?"

I nod.

"Why should I?" he says. "You don't even like me."

His words shock me. The sad look on his face is even worse.

"Mason . . . of course I like you. You're my little brother."

"But you never want to play with me. And you're always telling me I do everything wrong."

I'm about to object. But then I realize something. He's right. I *don't* ever want to play with him, because I'm too afraid of having my things messed up. And I *do* always tell him he's doing things wrong, because he doesn't do things exactly the way I would do them.

It dawns on me that I've been pretty mean to Mason. Especially during the last few weeks, when I've been so worried about the recital.

No dance, even a dance in front of Miss Camilla, is worth that.

I crouch down by where he's sitting. "I'm

sorry, Mason," I say. "I haven't always been very nice to you. I just like having things a certain way. And I get upset when other people . . ."

I'm about to say, *mess them up*, but I realize that's not fair.

". . . do things differently. But you're my little brother, and I care about you a lot."

He looks at me with his big brown eyes. "Really?"

I nod.

Mason reaches up and hugs me. I hug him back, hard.

Then I stand up to go.

"Wait," he says. "I'll teach you. If you still want."

I think about it. "Okay," I say. "But if I'm mean to you, you walk away. Deal?"

"Deal," he grins.

Chapter 12

We go back into my room, since it's bigger, and close the door.

"Wait a minute," Mason says. "Before we start, you've got to promise you won't tell anyone I can dance. Because ballet dancing is for girls."

I decide that now is not the time to point out that Mr. Lester isn't a girl, and that there are a bunch of older boys who take ballet at the Nutcracker School. "I won't tell. Promise."

"Okay," he nods. "So, you start with your right leg."

I stand behind him and stand on my right leg. We join hands and walk, then chassé. He turns to do the pirouette, but I get lost.

"Like this, Jerzey," he says. "Right foot in front of left foot." He shows me, but when I try, I get the steps all mixed up, as usual.

Mason is very patient. That's one thing about little kids: they don't mind doing the same thing over and over. When he was little, he wanted Mom to read him *The Little Engine That Could* at least three times each night. He still finds one book he likes and reads it again and again. His tolerance for repetition is definitely a good thing now.

"No, put your right foot in front of your left. *Then* do the turn," he says, for the fifth time.

But even though he's patient, I struggle. It's just like in dance class. My heart starts pounding, and I feel all shaky. The more we practice, the worse I get. After he shows me one step ten times and I still mess it up, I finally crack.

"I just can't do it!" I yell.

Mason squints. "Are you being crabby with me?" he says. "Or are you just being crabby, period?"

"Not with you," I say. "I'm just mad at myself. I'm a horrible dancer. I'll never, ever get it right." I draw in huge breaths to try to stop from crying. I collapse on my bed, blinking hard. "Maybe I really should just drop out of ballet." The image of Miss Camilla's face pops into my head, but I shoo it away.

Mason stands quietly looking at me for a minute. "Want me to show you again?" he asks.

I shake my head. "I can't. Maybe later." But a little voice in the back of my mind says there's not going to be a later. This is the end of the line for the dancing disaster. I am completely, utterly hopeless.

Mason looks a little relieved. "Okay. Then will you play basketball with me?" he asks.

"What?" I ask, sniffling.

"Will you play basketball with me?" he repeats.

Play basketball? Me? He's crazy. But then I think, why not? I can't dance. At least I can try to be a good big sister for once.

I nod.

Hardly knowing what I'm doing, I wipe a tear away with my sleeve and pull on my pink coat. Mason gets his jacket from his room, picks up his basketball, and leads me downstairs.

"We're going outside," he yells to Mom and Dad.

We head to the basketball court silently, Mason dribbling the ball. Two of Terrel's big brothers are at the far end of the court as usual, shooting hoops. They wave at us and we wave back. It's cold enough that our breath looks like big puffs of cloud around us. I stick my hands in my pockets to keep them warm.

When we get there, Mason stands in the circle of light that floods the court and tosses the ball to me. "Catch," he says.

I surprise myself by actually catching it.

"Try dribbling it," he says.

I bounce the ball up and down on the asphalt. When it gets away from me, Mason runs after it and tosses it back. The ball makes a satisfying *thwack* when it hits the ground. I bounce it up and down, trying to keep it in the same place with every bounce.

"Toss it here."

I awkwardly toss the ball to Mason. He bounces it a few times, does a graceful spin, and swishes the ball into the basket. He does a victory dance and bounces the ball left, right, and everywhere as he comes back over to me.

He tosses me the ball. "Now you try it, Jerzey," he says.

I hold the ball still. "I can't do that."

"Sure you can. I'll try to block you." He stands in front of me, waving his arms. I duck around him, run to the other side of the court, and try the jumping spin he did. I miss the basket, but not by too much.

"There you go!" he says. "Try it again."

I do, and this time I move more smoothly. I still don't make the basket, though.

He gallops around me. "Now, this is what you do if there are people trying to block you. You have to face them."

I run alongside him, the cold air rushing past me. Mason makes a face, and I crack up.

He does a fancy spin, flicking his leg out as he dribbles. "Bet you can't do that."

"Bet I can," I say, grabbing the ball and doing what he just did. He tries to get the ball away from me, but I spin around to stop him, then toss it neatly into the basket.

"I did it!" I cry.

He smiles. "That was real good, Jerzey. But I bet you can't do *this*."

He grabs the ball and takes three long steps, jumps, does a spin, and flicks the ball into the basket.

I grab the ball, dribble it away from the basket, and turn to face him. "Oh, yeah? Watch *this*."

I take three long steps, too, then jump and do the spin. I don't quite get the ball into the basket. But I'm close.

He takes the ball, bounces it to center court, and does the same moves again, except this time he adds a leap after he shoots the basket. He offers me the ball. Without a word, I take it. Gallop, spin, toss, catch, leap. This time the ball swooshes into the basket. I do Mason's victory dance. I'm out of breath, and my heart is pumping like crazy. And I realize I'm happy for the first time in what seems like weeks.

Mason stands there staring at me. "Hey, Jerzey! You did it."

I dribble the ball. "Yup. I'm a basketball star now," I say.

He shakes his head. "I mean, you did a bunch of your dance!"

I stop dribbling. "What?"

"Not exactly in the right order," he says, "but you can do all the moves."

When I continue to stare uncomprehendingly at him, he sighs.

"Don't you get it? The gallops are almost exactly like those—what do you call them?— the sashays."

"Chassés?"

He nods. "And the spin with a leg flick is almost that peer thing."

I realize he means *pirouette*. I finally catch on. "You mean . . . I really can do all those moves?"

"Sure you can," he says. "Maybe you just get all freaked out because you think you're bad at it. But you probably didn't think you were bad at basketball, because you'd never done it. I must be one really great teacher." He smiles proudly.

I am so thrilled to find out that I *can* do it, I really *can*, that I run over and give him a huge hug.

"Eww! Jerzey! Cut it out!" he hollers, glancing across the court at Terrel's brothers, who are grinning at us. But I think he's really not as mad as he sounds, because on the way back home, he reaches out and takes my hand.

"Thanks," I say as we climb the steps. "You saved my life."

"No problem," he replies. "But it's our secret, right?"

"Right," I say. "Definitely our secret."

Chapter 13

Over the next few days, I practice the dance in my room. I practice a *lot*. Mason comes in and helps sometimes. But what he taught me must have stuck in my head, because I can actually remember the steps now.

And whenever I start to get frustrated, I just imagine I am hanging out with Mason on the basketball court, trying to one-up him by doing higher jumps or longer gallops. I keep thinking of the cold air rushing against my face, the clouds of breath hanging around us, and the fun we had.

I hate to admit it, but I don't have fun a lot. I feel *satisfied* when my pencils are lined up just right, or when a new book is exactly the right size to fit into an empty space on my bookshelf. And I *like* being with my friends, for instance, when we all go to Bella Italia, Epatha's parents' restaurant, and eat garlic bread and talk. But I don't laugh very much. I think about things too much, and I get tied up in knots, and I worry.

So, fun is kind of new for me. I can tell Epatha has fun when she dances. It's as if she's using the dance to tell everyone a little bit about herself. I never would have thought that I could feel as though dancing were fun.

But maybe I can.

Before the next class, I march up the stairs to the studio with more purpose than ever before. For once, I'm not scared that I'll be awful. For once, I know the steps cold.

I can hardly wait for the moment when we break up into groups to practice our dances. The Rainbow girls go first. Their dance looks great, except for one part where a banner flutters the wrong way and trips Terrel. She gives the banner the scariest look I've ever seen. I'll bet it won't dare trip her ever again.

"Wonderful, girls," Ms. Debbé says as the music ends and they take their bows. "Now, Princesses."

She presses the button on the CD player, folds her arms across her chest, and waits.

The music starts. Jessica, JoAnn, and I join hands and walk in a circle. Then we do the chassés.

It doesn't take long for my sisters to realize that something's up. Jessica is ready to push me gently in the right direction for the pirouettes—but I go in the right direction on my own. JoAnn braces herself for the moment when I usually crash into her after the leaps—but I move smoothly past her, just like I'm supposed to.

I sneak a peek at the other Sugar Plums. Terrel's eyes are about to pop out of her head.

Epatha gives me a huge thumbs-up. Brenda looks around nervously, as if maybe she had accidentally slipped into a different version of reality and needed to find a way back home. And Al just beams.

When we finish, the room fills with cheers and clapping. Epatha lets out a hoot so high and loud I think the window's going to shatter. "*Fabulosa*, my friend," she says. "I didn't think you had it in you."

I have never seen Ms. Debbé look shocked before. But she looks shocked now. "Jerzey— however did you learn so much so quickly? Your sisters, they helped you?" she asks. She looks questioningly at Jessica, who shakes her head, and JoAnn, who does the same.

"Uh . . ." I look over at Mason, who's been watching the whole time. He shakes his head violently. "I guess I just finally got it."

I feel a tiny tug of guilt that I'm not being 100 percent honest, and that Mason isn't getting any of the credit. After all, without him I'd still be careening off the stage into people's laps. But he doesn't want me to tell, and frankly it would be embarrassing to admit that my seven-year-old brother is my ballet tutor.

Ms. Debbé doesn't question my answer. She just nods and says, *"Bien. Très bien,* Mademoiselle Jerzey."

And those five words from her mean more to me than anything anyone else has said.

Chapter 14

A few weeks fly by. Before I know it, it's the Tuesday afternoon just four days before our show.

Mom drops us off at the dance studio for our final costume fittings. All the classes are here at once, so there are kids everywhere. The kids from Ballet One are running around in the main studio shrieking at each other. A few harried parents try to get them to calm down, but it's impossible to keep a bunch of kindergartners in dragon costumes from racing around and breathing fire at each other.

Al calls to us from the top of the staircase. "Come on, you guys—Mom's up here." Al's mom is a designer and hatmaker. Our class's costumes have gotten decidedly more interesting since Al moved to town.

We thump upstairs, but it's so loud you can't even hear us. I cover my ears. I feel my shoulders start to tighten up—I'm not good with chaos, as you probably know by now.

"Come on," Al says again as we reach the top. She pulls me with one arm and Jessica with the other. "Wait till you see your outfits. You'll keel over."

We go into the second-floor studio. Al's mom is dressed in a sky blue suit studded with large, colorful fabric circles that puff out a bit. "We saw a balloon stampede on TV, and she got inspired," Al tells us. "There's a hat that looks like a hot-air-balloon basket, but it kept falling off whenever she leaned over to pin up a kid's costume."

Al's mom waves at us, then goes back to sewing up the back of Epatha's rainbow costume. It's really cool—a green bodysuit that covers her from the neck to the ankles. She looks like a green crayon, but in a good way.

"Come here," Al says. She's standing at a portable clothing rack where a bunch of long garment bags are hanging. "Look!" She unzips one of the bags and pulls out the most beautiful dress I've ever seen. Silver sequins shimmer on the pink top. Layers and layers of pink tulle float around it, forming the skirt.

"And you get crowns, too," Al says, pulling sparkly circlets out of a bag.

I can barely speak. "It's so beautiful," I breathe, touching the skirt.

JoAnn doesn't share my reaction. "You've got to be kidding me!" she says, shaking her head. I haven't seen JoAnn in a dress since our fifth birthday party. The last time Mom bought her a dress, she cut the skirt into two pieces and stapled them up the middle to make pants. Mom gave up after that.

Jessica elbows JoAnn. "Shhh," she says. "I think it's just lovely."

Al's mom comes up behind us. "I'm glad to hear it," she says, smiling. "I think it's pretty nice, too." She picks up the dress by the hanger and twirls it around. The tulle drifts through the air dreamily. "Let's try them on." She examines a tag in the dress. "Jerzey, this one is yours."

I take it and go into the makeshift dressing room, which is a curtain they've hung up on one side of the room. JoAnn and Jessica join me, carrying their dresses. I pull off my pink ruffled T-shirt and slip on the dress, then take my jeans off underneath. There's no mirror in here, so I can't see what I look like. But the dress fits perfectly.

We step past the curtain. Our friends gather around and admire us.

"You guys are the lucky ones this time," Al says, sounding the teeniest bit jealous. She got to be the Sugar Plum Fairy at the last dance recital, and her mom made her a gorgeous dress. But this one is just as nice. Even better, because it's pink, my very favorite color.

Jessica looks so pretty. She spins around and the skirt wafts out, then drifts gracefully down again. But JoAnn looks at her dress in horror.

"You gotta find your inner ballerina, girl-friend," Epatha says to her. "She's in there somewhere."

"She's probably drowning in all this pink stuff," JoAnn replies, picking up the top layer of tulle and dropping it experimentally, as though it was some substance that aliens just brought to Earth.

"Beautiful!" Al's mom exclaims. "You ladies all look terrific. Did you get to admire yourselves?"

I'd almost forgotten we're in a ballet studio—one of the walls is covered with mirrors. I race over, with Jessica right behind me. The dresses are perfect. We look like twin princesses—well, almost twins, since I'm skinnier and Jessica has her special ballet shoe on.

"I can't wait," I say to her as we face the mirror together, with matching grins on our faces.

"Me, either," she says.

The other girls come up behind us in their brightly colored outfits. "It's gonna be a good show," Terrel says, smiling with satisfaction.

A little Ballet One girl comes in. "Are you guys the Princesses?" she asks.

"Yes," says Jessica.

"Mr. Lester wants to see you outside. He was afraid to come in on account of there maybe being girls in underwear here."

JoAnn snorts as we walk out.

Mr. Lester is waiting by the stairs. "Great news, girls," he says. "Ms. Debbé was so impressed with your dance that she's moving it to the very end of the program. That's sort of the place of honor, you know."

"Even after the big kids?" asks Terrel.

"Even after the big kids," Mr. Lester says. "You've done a really good job—especially you, Jerzey. Ms. Debbé told me your sisters didn't even help you. It's just amazing how things could fall into place like that for you."

Once again, I feel a little guilty, but I try to push it out of my mind. And once Jessica and I start talking about how good our dance will be, I manage to forget it completely.

That night, I sit in my room, under my pink canopy, and think about how different I feel now from the way I felt a week ago. I would have never believed there could be such a big change in a person in such a short time. The old me would have been sitting on my bed now, too, but she'd have been worrying about doing everything wrong in the recital. The new me *knows* the steps. To prove it, I get up, do the first part of the dance, and finish with a spin (or a spinning jump shot). I smile. Nothing's going to go wrong now.

Then a sharp yell echoes down the hall—it sounds like JoAnn—followed by a crash. Then there's nothing but silence.

Chapter 15

I race out of my room, nearly crashing into Jessica, who's doing the same thing. We run to JoAnn's room and find her lying on the floor, moaning softly. Mason comes in, eyes wide with worry.

Mom and Dad thunder up the stairs at the same time. "What happened?" Dad barks—it's a huge change from his usually dreamy demeanor.

"Tripped . . ." JoAnn says. "Leg hurts. Bad." She grimaces, closing her eyes in pain.

"I'll call nine-one-one," Mom says, running from the room.

It seems to take hours for the paramedics to arrive, but later Dad says it was really only five minutes. A short, pudgy guy and a tall, lanky woman come upstairs with a stretcher. The woman gingerly examines JoAnn's rapidly swelling leg and announces that it's broken.

JoAnn's skateboard is lying two feet away from her. It's obvious that she tripped on it. But Mom doesn't say anything. I guess part of being a good parent is knowing when not to say, "I told you so."

"What can I do?" Dad asks. "Can I get her anything?"

The guy says no, they just need to get her to the hospital.

"You all stay here," Mom says to Dad, Jessica, Mason, and me. "I'll ride in the ambulance and let you know what's happening."

The woman gently lifts JoAnn's shoulders while the man moves her hips onto the stretcher. JoAnn hollers, blinking back tears. Jessica, frozen by the door, looks very scared.

My stomach is doing flip-flops. "Is she going to be okay?" I ask the man.

He looks over his shoulder. "She should be fine," he assures me. "She just won't be doing any skateboarding for a while."

Mom walks beside the stretcher, holding JoAnn's hand. We watch as the paramedics carry her out the door and down the stairs, to where the ambulance is waiting. It's dark, chilly, and damp outside. It must have just stopped raining. The reflections of the ambulance's flashing red lights gleam in the puddles. It would be pretty if I weren't so scared.

The paramedics push JoAnn into the back of the ambulance. Mom ducks and climbs in beside her. Dad, Mason, Jessica, and I stand there motionless as the ambulance pulls away, sirens blaring. It's stupid, but I want Mom to turn around and wave good-bye to us, because that would make things seem like they were going to be okay. But she doesn't.

We go inside in silence. Dad seems at a loss. He's still holding the newspaper he was reading when JoAnn fell. He's twisted it up into a little tube, and just keeps twisting and twisting it. "Well," he says, "why don't you go play, and I'll let you know when your mom calls with any news?"

Play? Like we're going to play when our sister's in an ambulance. I love Dad, but, like I said, he can be a bit clueless.

"Can we just stay in your study with you?" Jessica asks.

He stares uncomprehendingly at the paper in his hands, as if he's wondering how it got there and why it's twisted up. "Ah," he says. "Oh, yes, of course. Of course you don't want to play now."

We all go into his study. The walls are covered with masks Dad has collected during trips to Africa with his students. Usually, I think they're exotic and cool, but right now they look menacing, glaring at us through their empty eyeholes.

Dad sits in his chair at the desk. Jessica slouches on the burgundy-upholstered bench against the wall. I sink into the thick oriental carpet.

Mason comes over to me. "Can I sit by you, Jerzey?" he asks.

He collapses onto the floor beside me, and I put my arm around him.

"It'll be okay, Mason," Jessica says.

Mom doesn't call. And doesn't call. "These things take time," Dad says, as if trying to explain things to himself as well as to us. After a while, Mason falls asleep against me, and Dad carries him upstairs and puts him to bed.

Finally the phone rings. JoAnn's going to need surgery to have the broken bone set. "You girls might as well get some rest," Dad tells us. "I'm sure everything will be fine in the morning."

As I lie in bed trying to go to sleep, I play the whole thing over again in my head. "She just won't be doing any skateboarding for a while," the paramedic had said.

And then I realize JoAnn won't be doing any dancing for a while, either.

Chapter 16

"That's an extreme way to get out of wearing a frilly costume, girlfriend," Epatha says. "Excellent cast color, though."

We're in the hospital two days later, next to JoAnn's bed—Mom, Dad, Jessica, Mason, Epatha, and me. JoAnn has an enormous, lime green cast covering her leg from thigh to ankle. It was a pretty bad break, the nurse said, and they had to put some metal pins in the bone to set it. "So I'm part human, part machine now," JoAnn tells Epatha with pleasure.

"Yeah, right. More like part human, part paper clip," Epatha says. We're all in much better moods now that we know JoAnn is going to be okay.

Mom stands up. "We're going to need to let our patient get some more rest," she says. "It's been a very social afternoon."

Al, Terrel, and Brenda have already been here. Al's mom brought them all by right after school. Brenda was very interested in all the beeping medical equipment surrounding JoAnn. She wanted to know exactly what type of fracture JoAnn has and exactly how they fixed it. When the doctor came in to examine JoAnn, Brenda grilled her with so many questions that the doctor said she felt as if she were back in medical school. Then Epatha and her big sister, Amarah, came two seconds after the other girls left.

We all stand up to go—all except Dad, who's going to stay with JoAnn. "Hey, guys," JoAnn says to Jessica and me, "I'm sorry about the dance show. I guess I wrecked it for you."

"Oh, goodness!" Mom says. "I'd completely

forgotten. I'll call Mr. Lester the minute we get home."

As we walk out into the gray late afternoon, I think about the dance. I'm trying really hard not to be disappointed about it, because the important thing is that JoAnn's okay. But I feel tears start to form in the corners of my eyes anyway. I was finally going to get to wear a pretty costume. And I was going to be a good dancer, for the first time in my life.

A snowflake drifts down from the sky as we walk home.

"Snow!" Jessica says. It's the first snow of the season.

We all stop and look up. The streetlamps have just come on, and the snowflakes dance in their light—first just a few, then more and more.

If only there were a way to do our dance without JoAnn. But it's definitely a three-person dance. It would look stupid and unbalanced with only two.

"I caught one on my tongue!" Mason says, spinning around with his mouth hanging open, trying to catch another. "Look!"

That's when I have my idea.

Chapter 17

"Oh, no. No way," Mason says, arms folded defiantly.

As soon as we got home, I'd grabbed Mason, pulled him upstairs, shut the door behind us, and explained my plan. If he does the dance, the show can go on. And I can also come clean about not learning the dance by myself, which I've been feeling worse and worse about as everyone continues to treat me like some ballet miracle girl.

"But it'll be fun!" I say. "You'll get to be onstage in front of a whole bunch of people! Just like . . ." I grope for some comparison that will entice him. "Just like an NBA player."

Mason exhales. "I've never seen an NBA

player dressed like a stupid princess," he says. "And you haven't, either. Besides, you promised you wouldn't tell anyone I could do that dance."

I bounce up and down on my toes. "I *haven't* told anyone. But you could save the day. You could be a superhero, like Superman."

Mason shakes his head violently. "Superheroes do not dance," he says.

"Oh, yes, they do," I say, thinking quickly. "They have to learn to dance, in case they need to spy on bad guys at fancy balls."

He looks as if he may be considering this. "Even if they do, they don't wear dresses."

Oops. He's got that right.

"What if . . ." I stop and think desperately. "What if the dance isn't the Three Princesses? What if it's Two Princesses and a Handsome Prince? Or a Handsome Knight?"

I've got his attention.

"A Robo-Knight?" he asks.

"A Robo-Knight," I say firmly. "A very handsome Prince Robo-Knight who wears a cool costume."

He contemplates this. "What *kind* of costume?" he asks.

"Something really great," I say. "Girls love knights," I add, to distract him from my lack of concrete costume ideas. "And they love dancers. Remember how Epatha says she wants to dance at her wedding?"

I can tell he's wavering.

"I'll bet she'd think you were really handsome in a Prince Robo-Knight outfit," I say.

"Really?" he says.

"Really," I reply firmly.

He thinks for another minute. "Okay," he agrees. "I'll do it. But no stupid frilly things. And nothing pink."

I race down the stairs, Mason at my heels. "Mom!" I yell. "Don't call Mr. Lester yet!"

Chapter 18

Mason shows Mom the dance. She's astonished at how good he is and calls Ms. Debbé immediately. It takes some convincing to get Ms. Debbé to agree to the last-minute personnel change for our dance, even after she learns that Mason taught me the steps. It's a

good thing Mom's career as a lawyer gives her lots of practice at talking people into things, because that's what gets Ms. Debbé to agree.

But that isn't the only problem. Getting a Robo-Knight costume together in one day is not going to be easy.

After school the next day, all the nonhospitalized Sugar Plums meet at Al's house. We stand in the sewing room, and Al's mom gives us instructions. I cut fabric, because I am neat. Terrel organizes. Brenda analyzes the best way to cut up the silver plastic sheeting we found in

order to make knight armor. Al runs and brings supplies to each of us, because she knows where everything is. Jessica helps with the hand-sewing because she is careful and doesn't mind doing repetitive things like making tiny little stitches. And Epatha keeps Mason out of our way until it's time for his fitting.

Finally the costume is ready. Al's mom helps Mason into his leggings and his armor with the built-in robot control panel. She places his helmet, complete with antenna, on his head.

"Wow," he breathes, as he admires himself in the mirror.

"Can you dance in that, Mason?" Al's mom asks. He executes a neat pirouette. She laughs and shakes her head. "Amazing."

That night, when we're supposed to be in bed, I realize that this is the second time Mason's saved me. Without him I wouldn't know the dance. And without him, we wouldn't be able to dance in the recital.

I tiptoe into Mason's room. His lights are off, and I wonder if he's already asleep.

"Hey, Mason," I say.

"What?" he says sleepily.

"Thanks for saying you'll do the dance. It means a lot to me."

"You're welcome, Jerzey," he says, rolling over.

In just a few seconds I hear his even breathing. He's asleep already. In the dim light I can just make out his chest gently rising and falling as he breathes.

"I love you," I say, really quietly, so he won't hear.

The form in his bed shifts. "I love you, too," he replies.

I freeze, then smile and tiptoe out of the room.

Chapter 19

"Please hurry, Mason. We're on in just a few minutes," Jessica says.

It's the night of the recital, and we're in one of the classrooms getting our costumes on. Well, getting *Mason's* costume on. Jessica and I have been dressed for ages, but Mason insisted on going out into the audience to watch the other girls do the Rainbow dance.

"She was great," he says as he struggles with his shirt buttons. We don't have to ask: we all know he means Epatha.

The Rainbow girls join us. "Good luck, you guys," Al says.

Jessica turns to me. "Ready?" she asks.

I nod.

"How about you, handsome Robo-Knight?"

"Yup," Mason says.

"Then let's go." Jessica leads us out the door, down the hallway, and to the area behind the stage. We can see out into the audience. Mom, Dad, and JoAnn are in the front row. JoAnn's cast is sticking out in front of her, so green that it nearly glows in the dark. Miss Camilla is in the front row, right beside them.

Onstage, the older girls who are dancing in the number before ours are nearly finished. When their music ends, they curtsy and leave the stage. Mr. Lester walks on, looking a little discombobulated.

"Ladies and gentlemen," he says, "thank you again so much for joining us here tonight at the Nutcracker School of Ballet. There's been a slight change in the program. The final dance, instead of the Three Princesses, is going to be Two Princesses and Prince

Robo-Knight. Mason Deene will be dancing the part of the prince."

Backstage, Mason gives a satisfied nod.

Jessica, Mason, and I walk onstage and join hands. Our music begins. We do chassés and leaps, turns, and jump shots—well, ballet jump shots. We move in a circle, our right hands joined, as if we're dancing around a maypole. Mason has a huge grin on his face, and Jessica winks at me.

Before I know it, the dance is over. As applause fills the room, Jessica and I curtsy, and Mason executes the manly bow that we taught him last night. Ms. Debbé looks a bit faint, but happy, and Mom, Dad, and JoAnn are clapping so loud I think their hands may fall off.

When people start to leave, we go out into the audience.

Miss Camilla nods at me, a big smile on her face. She doesn't say a word. She doesn't have to.

"Did you have a good time?" she asks, turning to Mason.

"Mostly," he says. "Except the leggings itch."

"Your family is full of surprises," Miss Camilla tells Mom and Dad.

Mom looks from Mason to me. "It sure is," she replies.

Ms. Debbé joins us, along with the other Sugar Plums. "So, Mr. Mason," she says. "I wonder, do you think you might want to join a ballet class?"

Mason thinks about this. "I don't know. Maybe."

"We perhaps could have a special class for boys," she says.

"Then forget it," says Mason, looking at Epatha. "I'd rather dance with girls."

Chapter 20

After the show, we all go to Epatha's family's restaurant, where they've set up a huge table for us.

Epatha's parents have cooked up a pre-Thanksgiving feast. We eat spaghetti and stuffing, cannoli and cranberry sauce, eggplant parmigiana and pumpkin pie. It is weird but delicious.

Mom sits on one side of me and Mason on the other. "I didn't get a chance to tell you how good you were, honey," Mom says to me. "You did everything just right."

"Well, not really," I say. "I missed a step in the second part." I scoop up another bite of pie. "But that's okay. I had fun, and that's what counts."

Mom and Dad exchange a look. I'll bet they're wondering if the real Jerzey was kidnapped by aliens and replaced by a robot.

"Jerzey did really good," Mason says, between bites of cannoli. "She's a good student."

"You're a good teacher," I tell him.

"And a good dancer," Al says from across the table.

Dad leans back in his chair. "I think, given Mason's dancing and teaching prowess, he might deserve an early birthday present."

Mason jumps up. "Can I have my very own rat?"

"Yes," Dad replies. The rest of us groan. We didn't tell Mom and Dad about the rat incident. There are some things parents are just happier not knowing.

Epatha's mom, who looks like a movie star with her glossy black hair and bright red dress, stands up. "Since it's almost Thanksgiving, I would like to say that I am thankful you all could come and share this meal with us." She smiles and raises her glass. "To good friends."

Everyone joins in the toast, the grown-ups with their wineglasses and us kids with our sodas.

"I'm thankful for something, too," says Mason.

"What, cannoli?" asks JoAnn. "You've eaten about ten already."

"No, I'm thankful Jerzey made me do that dance, because it was fun. I'm glad she's my big sister. I'm even going to name my new rat after her."

My eyes start to prickle, but this time they're good tears. I manage to blink them away and say, "Thanks, Mason."

Mason picks up another cannoli. "And now Epatha knows I'm a good dancer, so she'll marry me."

Epatha watches the cannoli disappearing

into Mason's mouth. She squints skeptically at him. "Do you want to marry me because I'm nice, or because my mom makes good cannoli?" she asks.

Mason considers this. "Both," he says.

Epatha laughs.

"How about we see those dances again?" Epatha's dad asks.

I'm so full I can barely move. But he announces to the customers in the restaurant that we're going to do a show, and the customers start clapping. So we all stand up. Epatha's dad sings in a rich tenor voice, while the Rainbow girls dance with imaginary banners, and then Mason, Jessica, and I do our dance.

After we're all done, we line up to take a bow. I notice the line's not perfectly straight— I'm a little too far back.

It doesn't matter at all.

I join hands with my friends. "Another

triumphant moment for the Sugar Plum Sisters," Terrel says.

"And the Sugar Plum Brother," I add.

Then we sit back down and eat, till there are no more cannoli in sight.

Jerzey Mae's Guide to Ballet Terms
(With help from Mason)

barre—long railing that runs along the wall of a ballet studio. **When no one is looking, it's fun to hang upside down from it and pretend you're a bat.**

celery—crunchy green vegetable. Eating four stalks every day may improve ballet performance; however, this has not been tested, because all our celery got turned blue, by a certain person whose name I won't mention. **Jerzey, I *had* to! For school! How was I supposed to know you wanted that stupid old celery?**

chassé—sideways, galloping movement across the dance floor. Or the basketball court.

Epatha—the girl I am going to marry when I'm old, like, at least eleven. (That was Mason, not me. Obviously.)

Freeman, Miss Camilla—a very important ballerina who is elegant, talented, and refined. And her purse makes a good hiding place if you're a rat.

grand battement—large kicking movement. Why can't dancers just say "big kick"?

grand jeté—big jump. But not exactly like a jump-shot jump. See? That's why we need proper French terminology. How do you say, "whatever," in French?

plié—knee-bend. Miss Camilla did five hundred of these every day. Not recommended unless you like having spaghetti legs. Did you say spaghetti? I'm hungry.

pirouette—complete turn of the body on one leg. Jerzey used to be really bad at these until she went to Mason's Magnificent School of Ballet. No comment.

scarf, lucky—what Miss Camilla Freeman wore during all her ballet classes. Most effective if not previously used as a parachute for a toy soldier who landed in a mud puddle. Well, I couldn't just let him fall a million feet, could I?

sibling rivalry—when two kids in the same family (who have to, for instance, go to dance class together) fight a lot. Which Mason and I don't do anymore. Right. Even when I leave the cap off of your green felt-tipped pen and it dries out. *What?*